Dmitri: His Amazing Story

R. D. HUZUL

 FriesenPress

One Printers Way
Altona, MB R0G 0B0
Canada

www.friesenpress.com

There are so many people that I would like to thank for their ideas and contributions over the last couple of years during the compilation of the manuscript but unfortunately I can only give one huge thank to them all as space is limited . They know who they are and I am deeply grateful to them for their words and inspirational wisdom on this work. Each of them have earned a pat on the back as well as my utmost respect and admiration for their contributions.

ISBN
978-1-03-915164-2 (Hardcover)
978-1-03-915163-5 (Paperback)
978-1-03-915165-9 (eBook)

1. FICTION, HISTORICAL, WORLD WAR II

Distributed to the trade by The Ingram Book Company

Disclaimer

I do not condone the act of any kind of war. War is hatred. There are no real winners in war, there are just losers. As well, there is no place for prejudice, racism and bigotry. Sadly, humanity doesn't seem to learn from the evils of the past. God forgive us.

This story is about the experiences of a naïve young man drawn into a conflict through circumstances beyond his control. With a purpose in his heart and soul he seeks to pursue it. The purpose of freedom for his country, is what this young man sought, not any act of aggression. Unfortunately war was something he had to endure to pursue his passion.

foreword/Introduction

———

Life. It is said that the purpose of life is a life with purpose. This truly can be said of Dmitri Hrechko, the main character of this story. This fictionalized story based upon a real life person, reflects this throughout the novel. It is told as a memoir by the main character.

With total conviction, enduring commitment, immense courage and an unshakable faith, Dmitri endures the ravages of World War II to become a remarkable young man and a formidable leader. From humble beginnings, he responds to the challenges that present themselves to him with the decorum, grace and determination that didn't seem possible to a teenage boy. Yet, he overcame the obstacles through patience, persistence and perseverance. He quickly adhered to the values and characteristics of not only a good soldier but an excellent commander as well. Those values being integrity, loyalty, excellence, honesty, courage, responsibility, fairness and respect.

Throughout his amazing young life he made many true friends and gained the respect from those who knew him and loved him.

A famous quote comes to mind when referring to Dmitri. What John F. Kennedy, the 35th president of the United States, said at his inauguration in 1961 embodied the purposeful life of the young Dmitri Hrechko. President Kennedy said: "Ask not what your country can do for you – ask what you can do for your country." Indeed, Dmitri's love for his beloved Ukraine, permeated his soul and accelerated his desire for the independence of his countrymen. In reality, independence never happened.

His family, friends and the loving relationships of others motivated and inspired him, giving him the will and strength to continue his quest.

There are many themes throughout the story, notwithstanding that of love. Overwhelmingly, love could be considered the major theme of the story. Dmitri developed a great love and compassion for others despite the horrendous circumstances of a devastating war. The tragic loss of friends and comrades, while tumultuous, forced him to gain faith and inner strength he thought he never had.

To quote the words of the late Queen Elizabeth II, "Grief is the price we pay for love" (Quoted after the passing of Lady Diana in 1997). Indeed, Dmitri did grieve at the losses in his young life, but rejoiced at the love he did receive later in his life.

More than anything else, Dmitri developed faith to persevere. A strong and supportive family helped him develop inner strength, thus promoting his ongoing quest and purpose. With equanimity and strength of character he survived.

In the Bible, God says, "I will never leave you, nor forsake you." Indeed while being alone in his "amazing story", Dmitri never felt alone. He was guided throughout his journey. He found out what was and is truly important in life. His story is one that we can learn from.

Chapter 1:
Beginnings

As I reflect on my life and recall how my past shaped me, I cannot help but realize how faith instilled in me a sense of well-being and direction. Of course, circumstances beyond my control often intervened, but the friendships I developed in my younger years gave me the love and direction I needed to motivate me through the troubled times. As a result, I became increasingly grateful for the happier times. My life has been an amazing story of triumph over adversity and victory over defeat.

What is life? They say that life is what we make it. It can be uplifting and wonderful or it can be tragic and traumatic. The choice is always in our hands. We can embrace hope and happiness or we can be imprisoned by fear and despair. It is up to us to decide how we want to live our lives.

This is not a war story. It is a story of a person who endured and persevered from simple beginnings to one of ultimate fulfillment. It is a story of a person who coped with and survived the ravages of tragedy and then rose to uplifting triumphs. My name is Dmitri Hrechko and this is my story.

The Russian Revolution brought an end to the ruling elite Romanov family of the late nineteenth and early twentieth century. Massive social and political upheaval took place, changing the system in favour of the so-called working class. The Bolsheviks, under Vladimir Lenin and Leon Trotsky, sought to create a system that strived for the benefit of all.

With the change in ideology, reforms to the socio-economic system transpired. Centralization of resources and large-scale business interest consolidation and allocation by the Communist regime created a totalitarian state.

Under the authoritarian central regime of Lenin and then Joseph Stalin, the Soviet Union sought further unification of the republics under its sphere of influence. Unification by cultural destruction was undertaken by the Soviets. More atrocities were administered by the Communist regime, resulting in more famines and pogroms (mass killings).

Resistance to Soviet insurrection by the various once-independent republics, including Ukraine, proved futile. The republics were steadfast in their determination to resist but powerless to do anything about it.

In the midst of those changing times, I grew up in Western Ukraine. It was the late summer of 1939, and I was barely fifteen years of age when world events changed my life forever.

As a boy, growing up in Western Ukraine was a memorable time for me. My early years in the 1920s and 1930s, prior to World War II, were filled with adventure, wonder and happiness. After all, we were kids. We didn't know what was going on beyond our family farms.

The strong influences of political upheaval were rampant throughout the world. The League of Nations' failure to police global conflicts where despotic dictators were taking control of weak regimes in Europe, Asia and Africa led to mass insurrections and regime changes, causing instability in an already uncertain world. Rising anti-semitism in Germany also led to the largest genocide in history, which came to be known as the Holocaust.

For me, Dmitri Hrechko, my world was my home life with my parents (Julia and Ivan) and my friends and cousins. I was an only child. My friends and cousins were always close by if we wanted to play together after we finished our chores and our homework.

My family's farm was not very big. Although outsiders might consider us otherwise, we were content. We seemed to have enough to survive the long cold winters. We had a few cows for milk and meat, a small vegetable garden, and a few hectares of wheat or barley. Some of the crop was sold to local merchants and some was made into flour for us. My mom loved to bake and cook. The special holidays of the Orthodox calendar were always filled with the aromas and tastes of my mom's baking.

We had good times with my friends and cousins. Whether we were playing football (soccer), riding our horses–the old work horses loved being with us kids–or skiing and sliding down the mountain in winter, we had a lot of fun together.

Ivan, Yuri, Alex, and Slobodan were my best pals. Of course, some pretty girls hung around us too. We were teenage boys. What do teenage boys like? Teenage girls, of course. Then there was my cousin Maria.

Although Maria was a bit older than me, I still enjoyed being with her, and I was quite fond of her. When I looked at her, it literally took my breath away. She had long black silky hair with soft hazel eyes and a creamy complexion. I couldn't believe she was my relative. She was so beautiful. She had a soft, reassuring nature that always seemed to calm me down when I got mad, but I never got mad at her. Maria was so much wiser than any of us. She told us things about the outside world that we didn't know. Because she was an avid reader and an excellent student she knew information about various subjects. We all looked forward to her discussions with us on history, geography and science. She was like a school teacher to us, but we didn't mind; we loved being with her.

What can I say about Maria that hasn't already been said? She thought that I was a cute guy. She probably liked me as much as I liked her. She asked if I would like to have a girlfriend someday. I had never really thought about that. Going to school and looking after the farm with my parents were my biggest concerns. Things of a romantic nature hadn't come to mind yet, but that would change–all thanks to Maria..

Late one evening after our farm chores were done for the day and our gang had gathered for some fun, Maria took me aside. In Ukrainian she said, "Pishly zi mnoyu" (come with me) as she took my hand.

"I have to talk to you," she said to me in Ukrainian. We said goodnight to everyone else earlier than usual and then headed toward a backyard shed at Maria's place. We sat down together in a cozy corner. What was about to transpire seemed so natural, although it wasn't.

We were both confused about things that were about to happen or wouldn't happen. It could only be described as an epiphany. We just talked. I looked at her, and she looked at me.

"Scho ty khochesh vid mene zavaz?" I asked. (What do you want from me?)

"Ya ne znayu," she replied. (I don't know.)

"Ne dobre. Pohano," I said. (Not good. This is bad.) I added that we shouldn't be alone together in that place. However, we continued to talk for a while.

I thought I knew her, but I suppose I did not. Maria was a good girl. Her parents were good to her, albeit quite strict. She was an only child, like me, so maybe something was missing. I'm not sure if she had a boyfriend. Could that be it? Perhaps she couldn't find the affection she needed at home. While there was affection between us–she said that she always liked me–as second cousins, I couldn't and wouldn't allow things to go any further. She agreed. "Pravda, tak," she replied. (Truthfully, yes.) She knew it wasn't right. She gave me a quick peck on the cheek, and said "do pobachennya" (Goodbye). Then she left. I never saw her again.

Other things in the vicinity of my home village demanded my family's attention more than this. I needed to grow up and face the responsibilities that lay ahead, and I needed to do so in a hurry.

That night I learned some important life lessons about trust and respect, respect not only for others but also self-respect. Maria was my second cousin, and I loved her and respected her too much to take advantage of her good nature. Trust and a good reputation are hard to achieve but are easily lost with one misguided decision. I had much more difficult decisions and important life lessons ahead. Maria had taught me that.

I had more romantic encounters during my younger years. I realized that while my life was just beginning, I was having. I was having an epiphany in terms of what becoming a man is all about. It is and will always be understanding oneself, respecting oneself and others and taking responsibility for one's actions. Manifestations of these actions would definitely become evident in the forthcoming months and years.

When I arrived home later that evening, my mom asked me why I was so late. I told her that I had forgotten about the time. I was just having too much "fun" with my friends. I apologized and Mom forgave me.

Meanwhile, developments in the world around us were taking shape. It was the late summer of 1939, and Europe was on the verge of World War II. We had heard rumors of an invasion by Hitler in Poland. The Soviet Red Army was also preparing for war as it announced its visits to local towns. It needed men to equip the Russian war machine.

A feeling of fear and dread was in the air. I was starting to fear the outside world. It felt like it was closing in on my friends, my family, and me.

With the declaration of war, things were never going to be the same. My parents and I talked for hours about the seriously deteriorating environment, and what we were willing to sacrifice to preserve our lives. We feared for our homeland.

While talking about the impending threat to our lives, I asked my parents about their opinions and thoughts.

"Ya ne znayu," my father replied. (I don't know). Then he told me stories of what occurred after the Bolshevik revolution: mass starvations, mass killings, the pillaging of farms and villages. The result led to a traumatic existence for Ukrainians.

He said even before the Bolsheviks, Ukrainians felt like prisoners in their own homeland. He recalled ancient stories of Tartar and Cossack conquests and occupations and, of course, more recently in history, Russian rule under the regimes of Catherine the Great and other Russian czars. My dad then said to me, "Ya tebe lyublyu miy synu." (I love you my son.)

A sense of pride and a nationalistic identity was taking shape in me. What was becoming of my proud Ukrainian homeland? Growing up on a small farm in Western Ukraine, I only knew my tiny village and its surrounding region. In the autumn of 1939, I was a naïve fifteen year old adolescent when world events enveloped my simple life and brought them to my front door.

Ukraine felt similar to the other formerly independent Slavic and other republics of the USSR. Russia was in control and there was nothing we could do. I decided my fate with the help of my beloved parents. Interestingly, my mom was ethnically half German so we were a multilingual family. Not only could we speak Ukrainian and German, we could also speak Romanian because of our proximity to Romania.

German immigrants to Eastern Europe, particularly Russia and Ukraine, began in the late seventeenth century. Descendants of Anabapist, specifically Mennonites, immigrated from Germany to Eastern Europe due to persecution from the mainstream Lutheran faith. The split with John Calvin and Martin Luther over pacifism and church and state separation led to mass exile and expulsion for the Mennonites who were greeted with open arms later in the Russian Empire by none other than Catherine The Great, who interestingly enough, was German born.

The German exiles were allowed to retain their ethnicity and national identities while assimilating into the Russian and Ukrainian cultures. Many sought refuge in North America and South America, where their cultures have flourished to this day.

With the Bolshevik revolution in the early twentieth century, many Mennonites and German ethnics were forced out, either to North or South America and parts of Africa.

We knew what was coming. The Red Army was gathering young men in the various Soviet republics. Finally, when the Red Army arrived in our village, we realized we didn't have time to waste. Within hours of their approach, I told my parents that I wanted to leave. It was my decision. I knew it would devastate them, but I believed it was my cause. I told my parents that I loved them and gave them a big hug and kiss.

"Ya traba yiedem zaraz," I told my parents. (I must leave imme-diately.) With little more than the clothes on my back, a jug of water, and a loaf of bread, I fled. I had no certain destination in mind and little identification in my pockets, but I had begun my journey for freedom and the pursuit of a cause.

What were the alternatives? I had to make a choice. Was I willing to continue to live as a "prisoner" of the Soviet regime along with my countrymen or was I willing to stand up for freedom? It was an agonizing decision for me to consider. Interestingly enough, my decision was made clear for me in my young mind. Under Adolf

Hitler, the Germans had vowed to liberate the Sovietrepublics should the Nazis succeed in their war aspirations.

We were proud Ukrainians. We could never live under the totalitarian regime that the Bolsheviks had envisioned as fair and equal but was made worse under the horrors of Stalinist rule. We wanted to be free of the shackles of a communist dictatorship. This faint glow of hope, which had resonated in our hearts and minds for centuries, began to burn brightly in my soul. I had to fight. It would be my cause. I would find out the true costs of my cause in the next few years. As I discovered much later, in war, there are no winners, only losers.

Saying goodbye was the most difficult thing I ever did. I feared I would never see my parents or many Ukrainian and Romanian friends and family again, but I felt there was nothing else I could do. I had been forced to fight for a cause: my home and my life!

What will become of me?" I wondered. Could I do anything to advance my cause, to help win freedom for Ukraine?. Would I become just another victim of war? Who were these Germans? Was it true that they were seeking world domination? As for the Soviets, did they only want to suppress other cultures such as mine? I was too young to understand the mass propaganda being bandied about. All I had going for me was courage and determination. I just hoped those qualities would be enough.

Chapter 2:
From Boyhood To Manhood

Whoever says living in the bush country is an enjoyable experience should try it some time. It was a living hell. That was my experience upon fleeing from my home. Climbing down the Carpathian Mountains proved to be quite an adventure for a young man. Hiding by day, traveling at night, I needed to get as far away as I could in a short time. I was fortunate to find warm-hearted travelers who extended much-needed hospitality as well as a ride closer to Romania and places west.

Where was I going? I wasn't quite sure. My destination was uncertain. With luck, perhaps I could find a group of German soldiers whom I could join. My mission was getting clearer, but it still was not completely defined in my young mind. I just wondered why I was there. Was my cause realistic? I couldn't turn back now. I had to find my destiny. My homeland was on my mind.

Days from the Ukraine-Romania frontier, I was starting to run low on *kleb* and *voda* (bread and water). I thought I could survive longer on what little I took with me when I ran from home, never to see my parents, friends and family, and, especially, Maria again.

After walking for what felt like endless hours during the night, I laid down for a nap. I couldn't take a step further. I collapsed near a side road on the way through Western Romania. Luckily, the Russian soldiers didn't find me.

When I awoke I found myself in the warm caravan of a "Roma" family, otherwise known as Gypsies. They asked about my name and my identity and why I was traveling by myself across Romania. They warned me that the Russian army was not far away, recruiting for the "Motherland." I related my situation to them, and they soon realized I was someone who was determined to undertake his own "mission" in life, so to speak.

They were very hospitable to me. I was a total stranger, but an understanding between us developed over the next few days as we traveled northwest, from the Bucharest region. The language barrier between us wasn't great, although the Roma language was so different from anything I have ever heard before. It was not quite Slavic, nor was it romantic. Instead, it was a combination of different language families. For example, counting from one to three sounded more like a harmony than a verbal exchange. One was *ona para*, two was *dua para*, three was *tra para* and so on. There was something interesting and whimsical about them. The family who took me in consisted of one boy and one girl, both in their late teens, together with their parents. They were on their way across Romania with no particular destination in mind. Gypsies by their nature were nomadic and didn't really have a place to call home.

The boy and girl were friendly to me. In fact, the girl, Nadia, who was about eighteen or so, was smitten with me. I tried to resist her advances, but over time it became increasingly difficult. Her brother, Peter, saw what was going on and advised Nadia to calm down or else she would be not able to devote herself to supporting the family business.

The "family business" had several different aspects. First of all, they were craftspeople, creating small items such as tools, small and large knitted pieces, and other handmade pieces of clothing and metalwork. These crafts, along with a little sleight of hand in the local market places, enabled the family to survive. Of course, Nadia was an economic asset to the family. Let me just say that her customer service came with a price.

Days later, the frontier of Czechoslovakia beckoned. The gypsy family said they could not take me any farther. Once we entered Czechoslovakia, we parted ways, and I thanked them for their kindness. They wished me well and gave me enough bread and water to last several days. Nadia gave me a kiss, and I was on my own again, headed to Bratislava and beyond. I realized there was no turning back. I was on my own again in a strange new country.

I had learned a lot about Czechoslovakia's history in school, but what I saw fascinated me, especially the beautiful and stunning lifestyle of the people and the iconic buildings. Dating back several centuries, the Romanesque and Gothic architecture of the churches in particular left me awe-struck. Just a farm boy, I still admire what I saw in the towns along the rivers, in particular along the Danube.

After several days of traveling and keeping to myself, in the distance I saw a German convoy. It was what I had hoped for. It was what my pilgrimage to freedom was all about. Could the Germans be the liberators of Ukraine? My naivete clouded my better judgment, and by the time I found out, it was too late.

Within a few hours, I caught up to the convoy. It was heading through Czechoslovakia en route to joining other small convoys along the Danube River for a march into soon-to-be-occupied Western Europe.

When I reached the tail end of the convoy, a few of the troops who were taking a badly needed nap spotted me and yelled at me to stop where I was going.

"Halt, was macht tu?"

I told them who I was and what I was doing. The troops laughed at me at first but then saw the determined expression on my face.

They took me to their commanding officer, Major Steiner, who met me with a look of anguish. He couldn't believe a boy as young as me would make such an epic journey. He wanted to know about me, but I had little in the way of identification. I had fled home with only the clothes on my back and not much else. I told him that I was a Ukrainian national who also spoke German. I also told him that I had fled because I wanted freedom for my homeland, and I thought that Germany could and would provide that freedom. I told him I wanted to fight for my homeland's liberation.

He said he would impose conditions on me prior to enlisting with their unit. Their conditions were not acceptable to me, but what choice did I have? First, I had to pledge allegiance to the Third Reich and Der Führer, and second, I was to be held under armed guard overnight for observation by the troops. They brazenly showed off their machine guns and Luger in front of me. So, there I was, a prisoner in the clutches of the Wehrmacht.

The morning brought about change–and a revelation. Major Steiner was the first German soldier to welcome me into the Wehrmacht. "Komm her Soldat Hrechko, Willkommen im Dritten Reich" (Come here soldier Hrechko. Welcome to the Third Reich). I was overwhelmed. I felt like I was part of something important. I also felt I was fighting for a cause that I thought was right: Ukraine's liberation from the Soviet Union. Even so, I felt so alone there in that strange country (Czechoslovakia). I didn't know anyone but something kept me going. Whatever it was, it was building within my soul. This sense of wellbeing kept me going.

The convoy moved on. I was part of the German Wehrmacht now, the feared war machine that was quickly restocking provisions from the locals. The eastern part of Europe was increasingly under Nazis control, but the conquest of Russia was the unltimate goal. The liberation of my homeland was what I aspired to fight for. This aspiration kept resonating within me.

The next few days brought us into the middle of Czechoslovakia, close to Prague. We were to meet with a smaller contingent there. The rendez-vous would increase our numbers before crossing the Alps. A short time later, we found the smaller unit of several hundred troops and continued our westward march along the Danube.

Quaint farms and villages with thatched roofs and picturesque town squares were everywhere along our way. I was just a farm boy, but I was in awe of the beauty of Europe, especially the architecture of eastern Europe.

Outside of Prague, we needed a rest after marching for days. I took the time to familiarize myself with the other enlisted men. It wasn't long before I knew the "gang." There were some real characters among them, to say the least, including Werner Klump, Hans Eisch, Jan Smigler, and Heinz Schultz. These guys became my closest buddies. As young men and soldiers, we all got along well. We came from similar backgrounds: small rural towns–so we could relate to one another. Our togetherness was uncanny.

I got along best with Heinz. I literally bumped into him. He turned to face me and said, "warum?" (Why?) I said to him, "Tut mir leid." (I am sorry.) We became instant friends. He was a few years older than me, about eighteen to twenty years old. In addition to being best buds, we were also comrades in arms. Heinz stood apart from the other guys. His personality, his fun-loving nature, his boyish charm, his strength of character, and his sense of humor made him not only a good and loyal friend, but also like the brother I never had.

By late fall of 1939, it was getting colder. Dark days lay ahead. As the endless days of marching passed by, Heinz and I became inseparable. He taught me a lot of life lessons, especially regarding women and poker playing. I learned his mannerisms, his likes and dislikes, and his favorite phrases. When he talked about women for instance, he often said, "No skirt is safe." He said this with bravado to impress the other guys rather than to express any prowess he might have had in the ways of romance. He always was a true gentleman with the opposite sex.

Heinz was also a generous person. My initial impressions of him was that he would give his shirt off his back or even his life for a friend. He and I were inseparable pals. I suppose he and the others were also searching for a cause to fight for, or perhaps they were just looking for adventure and a paycheque to support their families. Maybe it was a little bit of both. I was certainly looking forward to the adventures that might come along.

As naïve young men and brave soldiers, we didn't know what to expect. The Third Reich's ulterior motives were beyond our youthful comprehension. However, we would all soon realize the traumatic consequences of Nazi decisions and repercussions for us as mere foot soldiers and for humanity in general.

Stopping in a local Czech town in order to take a well-deserved overnight break, a group of us went to a local drinking establishment to refresh ourselves. Needless to say, the locals were not impressed by our presence, but they realized their country was being occupied. I didn't think much of what was happening, but before I knew it, the boys brought me a beer and invited me to partake in a poker game. I was really getting an education in "real life." I didn't know how to play poker, but with Heinz tutoring, I became knowledgeable rather quickly.

The next day, we headed along the northwestern frontier toward Austria. Along the way, our first skirmish took place. A group of partisan snipers spotted our convoy and began shooting.

My mind suddenly flashed back to my younger days with my Tati (my nickname for my Dad). I vividly remember hunting with Tati. He taught me how to handle a rifle. I wasn't very good at first but with practice, my aim improved. He was an expert hunter. The local deer were always in fear of him, I am certain. I was so proud of him. He said he was proud of me when I shot my first rabbit. "Ya hordyy," he said. (I am proud). I loved Tati. He gave me the confidence I needed to grow. Maybe that's why I am here to fight for him and my country.

Then, I heard Major Steiner yell, "Schnell, schnell, schnell," (quick quick, quick) as he pointed to the surrounding trees. I didn't know how to handle a machine gun but I learned quickly.

In the grip of fear, I fired my machine gun aimlessly into the adjacent woods. Surprisingly, some snipers fell from the trees. I don't know if I had actually hit any of them, but I received some congratulatory hugs from my buddies afterwards.

Major Steiner praised everyone who took part in the skirmish, including me. Many soldiers received commendations for bravery. I was promoted to a corporal and beamed from ear to ear upon hearing this from our commander.

We continued our march westward. The colder days of winter were fast approaching.

The next frontier, Austria, was not far away. Once again, I was overwhelmed by the beauty of Europe. Austria was so spectacular, with the Alps in the distance and the majestic Danube before us.

Arriving in Vienna was like an experience unsurpassed in my young life. The sights and sounds of the city center and the glorious and magnificent gothic cathedrals and music halls were simply stunning. I could see why Vienna was so cherished by Germany. It was so beautiful.

We settled down for the night just north of Vienna. From our hilltop camp site, we could see the glittering lights of the Austrian capital and hear the wondrous strains of joyful classical pieces emanating from the many open-air music halls. It was like a lullaby wooing us to sleep. To me, it was magical.

Heinz's assessment of the situation was sharp. "Das ide wunderbar. Machen ein movie our dar plätze?" Sharp-witted Heinz even suggested that the place was so wonderful and beautiful that maybe someday a movie could be made about it. Maybe a movie would be made about his relection about this beautiful country of Austria.

The next few days found us heading west toward the Swiss and Italian Alps. The highest point in Europe beckoned us, Mont Blanc. We didn't know what was in store for us in Italy or Switzerland. Since the Swiss were neutral, our platoon chose to march on the Italian side of the Alps.

It was early winter 1940, and the days were growing shorter. Snow was falling daily, which hindered our progress.

Descending from the Alps into Italy proved difficult for some of the troops who were not familiar with mountaineering. Since I grew up in the Carpathian region of Eastern Europe, it was not difficult for me. The roads in Northern Italy were not easy to traverse, but we slogged along for kilometer after kilometer. Once we reached several hundred meters below the summit, we headed west through Northern Italy. Our convoy, which consisted of several tanks, supply trucks, and personnel carriers along with several hundred troops, was looking forward to a day or two of rest in a small Italian frontier town. After all, the Italians under Mussolini were on our side, or so we thought.

We stopped at a local tavern for the night, where we tried various types of food, including primo and segundo, and drank our fill of local beers and wines.

A card game ensued afterward, during which I learned something important about poker: poker players cheat. After the first hand finished, and more bets were on the table, saw Heinz slip an extra card into his hand. I didn't say anything, but one of the other guys noticed and mockingly pointed his pistol at Heinz. Heinz relented and returned the card. I thought he knew better, but he suggested it was just for fun. Ever the jokester, he made us laugh about it and all was forgotten that night. Interestingly enough, Heinz did win a game legitimately later on with a royal flush over four aces held by another close buddy of mine.

The next morning after a restful night we were on our way again. We were not too far out from the tavern when it happened... bam! A landmine exploded near the front of the convoy. The lead vehicle (*kugel wagen*) with Major Steiner in it flipped over. Steiner was severely injured. With that single knockout blow, our troops were essentially left without experienced leadership. A few of the troops were more senior than me, but I found myself suddenly taking on more responsibilities.

Major Steiner was taken back to town for medical care. He did not make it through the night. With Steiner gone, we had a leadership vacuum. A group of the senior officers formed a coalition to continue the march through the Alps into France. I was invited to listen in on their conversations.

Decisions were made quickly. I was given a role in the renewed march across the Alps. I realized the senior officers were using me for their own ends, but I figured it was for the best. Imagine that, a boy who was not quite sixteen taking charge. I was to lead a small contingent across a narrow pass into France. I was to be the sacrificial lamb, their guinea-pig, so to speak. I knew the mission would either make me or break me. I had to prove myself. What choice did I have? I had to abide by their decisions. I had to fight for my cause however fleeting it was. Desertion was not an option for me. The mission would be my making or my unmaking as a man. The next morning would tell the tale. *What am I doing here?* I wondered. *Do they want me to die because I'm nothing but an expendable teenager who doesn't really belong with them?* They didn't want me, I knew that.

Early the next morning, we began the long, slow crawl from northern Italy near the Po River toward the frontier of the French Alps. With daylight on the horizon, we could see the French Alps in the distance. However, we had no idea what was waiting for us on the French frontier. Would I survive? Would this be the end of my journey and my cause?

With the sun's rays beaming at us near the French border, we felt uneasy, weary, and nervous regarding what lay ahead. Our fears were confirmed much later. As my first group led the division into the narrow passes between France and Italy, shots rang out. It was an ambush. As the sun broke over the horizon, a barrage of gunfire began. We didn't know who was shooting at us. They could have been partisans or other anti-fascists. They could have been a contingent of "allies" doing surveillance and/or reconnaissance. However, within minutes our division gained the upper hand. Once again, our troops' superior training proved to be of extreme advantage.

Over the next couple of hours, although we suffered significant casualties, we made it through the pass into northeastern France. I couldn't believe what we had been through. Although I was not a deeply spiritual person, I thanked God for keeping us fairly safe from disaster. "Dankeschön Gat!!" I repeated to myself over and over again. "Dankeschön."

I also began to think about home. My mind flashed back to my parents as I wondered how they were doing. Later, I learned that things were not going well for my homeland or my family. My father was convicted for aiding in my betrayal of the Russian motherland. For his so-called crime, he was sent to a Siberian salt mine to work for the state. His right hand was also amputated so that he would be unable to fashion or operate any type of tool or weapon. It was a vicious reminder of the ruthless authoritarian control of Joseph Stalin's communist regime. My mom was sent to a collective farm in southern Ukraine. The farm's assets and livestock were liquidated by the regime to further the war effort.

I also thought about my friends and cousins. What happened to them? Much later I learned that my friends were abducted and sent into the Red Army while my cousin, Maria, was given the choice between military service and collective farm labor. She chose to become a farm wife, and she became involved with a local collective farm manager. *"Oh, Maria, why?"* I wondered. *What happened?*

With France on the horizon, I led my division safely through the Chamonix Izere region and northeastern France. Mont Blanc, the highest peak in the Alps, could be seen in the distance. Once again, I prayed, "Dankeschön Gatt!"

What happened next was a significant morale booster to only for me but also for my entire division. Apparently, just after our brief skirmish on the French border, the senior officers contacted headquarters to tell them what happened, the commanding officer in the French region, now occupied by the German invaders, contacted headquarters in Berlin with the result of the skirmish.

The leaders at HQ were astounded that our troops were led by a teenager–me. A commendation was in order, directly from Der Führer. When word of it filtered through the division, hugs and congratulatory handshakes abounded until our arrival in Val D'Isère.

Heinz, my best buddy, was the first soldier to offer his best wishes to me, a reluctant hero. "Wunderbar, wunderbar mein freund," he said. To my surprise I became a lieutenant as a result of this successful offensive. The good wishes and congratulations continued well into the evening once we settled in Val D'Isère.

Suddenly, I began to experience excruciating pain. I didn't know what it was, but I was exhausted, and all I wanted to do was die.

Chapter 3: French Misadventures

As our troops settled into Val D'Isère for a rest, I collapsed near our accommodations. Several senior officers and troops took me to a local physician. After being woken at gunpoint, the French doctor reluctantly agreed to treat me in his office.

Tearing open my shirt, which was already torn due to being trapped under my vehicle during the Alps attack, the physician discovered a laceration on my upper-right shoulder. I didn't realize it, but I had been shot, and the bullet had penetrated lodged into the muscle, which was why I didn't have significant bleeding. I guess I was just damn lucky. If it was any deeper, it could have severed any artery. I gave thanks again to a higher power. "Dankeschön, Gott!"

The doctor bandaged me up and gave me some pills for the pain and to prevent infection. Our officers thanked the reluctant physician for his kindness, and the doctor grudgingly accepted the gratitude from his unexpected evening visitors.

A few days later we were marching west again when we encountered another group of German soldiers on their way toward the

French capital. The entire entourage was ordered to march into Paris as a demonstration of German supremacy.

Soon, our division (the 6ᵗʰ Wehrmacht) could see the spectacular capital of France in the distance, including the Eiffel Tower and the Arc de Triomphe. I had heard about the significance of these structures to not only the French but also to Europeans in general. Now I understood why the Third Reich wanted to capture Paris quickly and painlessly with minimum destruction and maximum preservation. It was a beautiful sight to see. I was quite in awe and filled with pride to be there.

For the next several days, our division remained in and around Paris. Under the supervision of headquarters in Berlin, the remaining top officers in our division told us that to better serve the interests of the German occupation of France, it was necessary to learn as much as possible about French culture. At the very least, that meant the top officers were expected to learn French as well as some English. Intense training ensued over the few weeks with our top officers quickly adhering to French culture in various ways. Basic phraseology was utilized with an emphasis on interrogation procedures for those who intended to pursue vocational training for Gestapo and SS positions. I decided to take part in the additional training procedures. I thought it might be fun, and I enjoyed learning new things.

After a few weeks, I was able to speak several French phrases easily, as was Heinz. He loved to have fun with the group. During the French-immersion period, he led us to the best nightclubs and cafés in Paris. He seemed to know where to go and to have a knack for that. He also considered me as one of the boys. Late in 1939 when I first joined this group, the rest of the group did not think much of me and thought I was just a naïve, stupid kid who was looking for adventure (probably like some others in the division). Over time, however, I had proved my worth to the group. After all, I had received a commendation from the higher-ups including the

Führer himself. I felt like I belonged! Did I belong there though? In my mind, I was still deeply puzzled. Did I want to belong here? I had my doubts, but I was there for a cause–Ukraine, of course.

Being a lieutenant meant getting respect from the others, but to Heinz I was still just one of the boys. "Kommen sie heir mein freund!" (Come here, my friend.)

"Certainement mon ami, allons-y moi a la café dans Paris a regardé les mademoiselles toute suite. N'est-ce pas?" I replied in French, so I could practice my linguistic training. (Certainly, my friend, let's go to downtown Paris and see the ladies, quickly, OK with you?)

Heinz's favorite reply was that "No skirt was safe with him." I already knew that. Even though he always said that in jest. Heinz was a decent, caring young man. He definitely was not the devilish skirt chaser that the other guys thought he was. That was just bravado. Heinz wouldn't harm a flea.

After a few nights of drinking and fooling around, I'm sure that Heinz and the boys had had enough of the many "pleasures" that Paris had to offer. I know I had. I wanted something else. Needless to say, the French were not very hospitable hosts. They made it clear we were not welcome in France! Nevertheless, they had to tolerate us despite their repulsive actions toward us and vice versa.

Not long after our language-training period concluded, another interesting and rather exciting opportunity came about. The Luftwaffe needed to train additional pilots in the event of an invasion by overseas enemies as well as a potential aerial assault on England (later known as the Battle of Britain.) As soon as I heard this, I had to sign up. I suppose I craved the excitement of being a "flier." *A Luftwaffe pilot, I thought. Wow, what a thrill that would be!*

The training course over the next couple of weeks was intense. I learned the fundamentals of flight, and I was ready to take to the skies, to attain my "wings." Training with a flight instructor in a training biplane gave me the confidence after a couple more days to go solo.

On the morning of my solo flight, I got up before the crack of dawn, undertook my pre-flight checklist, checked my instruments, then prepared my flight plan, which would take me over Paris. I thought I was ready to join the ranks of the Luftwaffe. What could go wrong?

I took off from the airfield toward downtown Paris. Within the hour I was flying over the fabled Seine River. I felt so joyous and free, like a master of the sky. Below, I saw where our division was stationed. Something I saw distressed me, however: caravans of German trucks rounding-up people along the city streets. Something strange was going on. Something I did not understand. I kept flying along the Seine, but what I had seen really bothered me. I didn't think it was right. (This strange activity would be later known as the Holocaust where some millions of innocent Jewish people were killed in mass extermination camps in Eastern Europe. It was the most horrific genocide in human history!)

What was going on along the streets of Paris? The uncertainty of not knowing what was happening had an effect on my flight vector. I wasn't thinking straight. I dropped lower to observe. I was heading toward the Pont des Artes and Pont Alexandre III (the Bridge of the Arts and Alexandre Bridge) when something else caught my attention.

Ahead of me on Pont Alexandre III appeared to be a Gestapo agent. I could tell that he was with the revered enforcement and intelligence branch of the Third Reich due to his uniform. His distinctive black military garb with a swastika emblazoned on each arm clearly identified him. What was he doing there? Was he waiting for a rendez-vous with someone? When he saw me, he motioned toward my aircraft.

I nosed my plane lower toward the bridge. The Gestapo agent began waving his arms at me even more energetically. As

I approached the bridge he attempted to jump up to catch my plane's left wing. He almost made it but he couldn't hold on. His hands slipped off my left wing tip, and he fell in the river. I felt like I had failed him. It was unexpected and there was nothing I could have done to help him. Fortunately, the river was fairly shallow, and the Gestapo agent managed to swim back to shore after failing in his "rescue" attempt. Relieved, yet somewhat perplexed as to what had transpired. I set a course back to the airfield at Orlys. I wasn't supposed to be here. It wasn't a rescue mission on my part. Gosh, I couldn't believe how stupid I was for doing that.

Within the hour I was back at the airbase. A reception committee was waiting for me. They didn't look very friendly. I had felt so exhilarated and giddy while in the air that I had neglected to adhere to my flight plan, and I went off course several times. I guess it was my adventurous spirit that made me do it. I also wanted to show off to my buddies. I was still very much a kid even though I had been entrusted with the safe operation and maintenance of a Luftwaffe aircraft. Well, what do the French say? "C'est la vie! That's life." So what?

Two Gestapo agents brandishing Lugers escorted me to the section commandant's office.

"Das ich schizen! Nix Gate. Sie ein dummkopf!" (This is crap! Not good. You are a goofball!) Many other not so wonderful German expletives were hurled at me. The commandant was not happy with me, to say the least. *Tell me how you really feel,* I thought. He really lambasted me for my stupidity. Yes, I admitted it to him that I had committed an error in judgment, to put it mildly. "Warum?" he asked (Why did you do what you did?)

The interrogation continued for a couple of hours, though it felt much longer as the commandant continued his tirade. The two Gestapo agents glared at me as though I had done something with criminal intent. In fact, I admitted I had done something stupid. I felt like a puppy dog who had just been caught tearing up the sofa cushions, my head lowered and my proverbial tail between my legs.

The commandant summed up his frustration with a demand for an apology. "Lieutenant Hrechko, you failed to follow your flight plan and you interfered with a military.Intelligence operation by attempting to retrieve Gestapo agent Schiller on Pont Alexandre III . You have humiliated me and made me look ugly as a commandant." The commandant said it in perfect English because he was very annoyed with me and because he felt he needed the practice, just in case I didn't completely understand him in German regarding the drastic circumstances of my actions.

I didn't know what to say, but I knew I had to say something to defend myself while at the same time ingratiate myself toward the commandant. After all, he was a decent person, and I respected him as a leader. Somehow my apology didn't seem sufficiently remorseful or forthright, like I intended it to be.

"OK, OK, OK," I said, "I'm sorry you're ugly." Befuddled by my own remarks, I looked at the commandant for any sign of appeasement. Instead, he glared at me in disgust and then demanded a real apology from me.

He was too stoic to acknowledge my pathetically stupid apology. The Gestapo agents smirked to themselves.

The commandant finally calmed down. "Tell you what I'm prepared to do for you, Lieutenant," he said. "You have demonstrated exceptional leadership skills despite your youthful inexperience. While I do realize you possess an incredible sense of curiosity, I believe that your leadership ability and your thirst for knowledge can be better utilized elsewhere in the service of the Third Reich. It is obvious to me that you have, as the French would say, a *penchant* for observation and interrogation. That being said, we require more personnel in the Provence region of France who are capable of undertaking observation and surveillance missions with the SS and the Gestapo. Therefore, Lieutenant Hrechko, you will train there as a surveillance officer. If you are successful, you may have the opportunity to become a member of the Gestapo or SS. You will leave for Marseilles tomorrow."

Feeling both ambivalent and elated about the decision, I thanked the commandant for his generous offer. Quite frankly I expected a more severe reprimand.

When I returned to my home base, the boys were thrilled to see me. Heinz was the first one to greet me.

"Was mach-tu, mein freund?" (How's it going, my friend?)

I told him that the interrogation went better than I had expected. The commandant thought I was being funny with him. He said I was a better soldier than a funny guy. (In today's parlance, that could be translated as "Don't quit your day job because you're not as funny as you think you are.") Heinz suggested that all of the boys should go out to a local drinking establishment to celebrate. I couldn't help but wonder what Heinz had planned.

"Let me guess," I said in English. The commandant insisted that I speak more English and French to enable me to communicate more effectively with the locals in my forthcoming new assignment as a surveillance officer trainee.

"I suppose you're heading to an establishment where there is a significant number of fräuleins or mademoiselles, mon ami, n'est pas?"

"Yah, yah, das ist richtig," Heinz replied. (Yeah, yeah, that's right.).

"Do I need to notify the local authorities of your presence?" I asked.

"Why?" Heinz blurted.

I couldn't help but state the obvious. "Well, Heinz, you always stated that no skirt is safe with you!" I knew that Heinz was a fun-loving guy. He was harmless. He liked to kid around with us, that's all.

"Richtig! Richtig!" Heinz countered. (You're right! You're right!)

27

We had a lot of fun that night. Heinz was a colorful character, and I didn't know if I would ever see him again. I kept thinking about how he had touched not only my life but also the lives of everyone around me. He was loving, caring and considerate of others, exactly what a friend should be.

The next morning I was enroute to the south of France, accompanied by several supply and troop vehicles.

Once again, I didn't know what lay ahead. Fear and anxiety gripped my mind. I had no idea who I was at that point. Was I a true Ukrainian willing to sacrifice myself for my homeland, or was becoming something else that I never intended to be? My homeland was still vivid in my mind.

That's why I'm here! I told myself. *Slava Ukrina.* (Proud Ukraine homeland.)

Chapter 4:
For The Love of Madeline

By the end of the day, our unit stationed itself on the outskirts of Marseilles. We set up our headquarters in a former hotel. After a dinner break with the personnel, I spent the rest of the evening familiarizing myself with the local area.

While I was in Paris, I had taken lessons on a motorcycle so that getting around places such as Provence and Marseilles might be easier for me. I hadn't expected to use my skills so quickly, but then again, I wasn't much of a drinker, so while the others were drinking and carousing, I focused on learning how to drive a motorcycle.

As the days passed, I was becoming more accustomed to my new duties as a trainee in the Gestapo. I was also quickly acclimatizing to the South of France. It was the spring of 1940, heading into summer. It was a very welcome change for me. I had never seen palm trees before.

The German air campaign has some early success in surprise air raids on Britain, known as the Battle of Britain, but by the autumn of 1940, the tide was turning in favor of the Allies. Britain and its allies managed to withstand the Luftwaffe's onslaught. In addition, the supply lines from Germany to the British shores proved to be too far away, thus providing yet another Allied advantage.

When I heard those reports, a sense of peace and relief settled over me. *Maybe, it just wasn't for me,* I thought. I also thanked God once again for sparing my life and prayed for my colleagues who had volunteered to join the Luftwaffe. I hoped that some of them had survived.

Other things bothered me as well, such as what was happening in my homeland and what was happening in the streets of Paris. I wouldn't know those truths until the end of the war. I tried talking to my superiors about the mass roundups I had witnessed in Paris, but the only answer my superior officers would give was that the people I had seen rounded up were taken away to evacuation camps where they would be "safe" from certain dangers in the city.

I tried to maintain a sense of confidence and decorum during my daily patrols, assuming a positive attitude despite what was happening around me. I needed something to help me feel good again.

One day while on my morning patrol in the south sector, I saw exactly what–or, rather, who–I was looking for. Her name was Madeline.

She was standing along a long gravel road that led toward a villa over rolling fields of vineyards. I pulled up beside her. "Bonjour mademoiselle! Je m'appelle Lt. Dmitri Hrechko, division sixième, Wehrmacht aus Deutschland dans Le Sud du France." (Good day, Miss. My name is Lt. Dmitri Hrechko, Sixth division, Wehrmacht Germany in Southern France).

"Mon plaisir à vous rencontrer, Lt. Hrechko," Madeline replied. (My pleasure to meet you, Lt. Hrechko). "Je m'appelle Madeline Savoy."

"Il fait beau aujourd'hui, n'est pas?" I continued, trying to make small talk. (Nice day today, isn't it?)

"Certainement, mais peut j'assiste toi avec quelle choses maintenant?" Madeline replied. (Certainly, but can I help you with something now?)

"Ne pas necessaire, Mademoiselle." (Not necessary, Miss.)

Our conversation continued for a brief period before I took the hint and continued my patrol rounds, but I returned again the next day to see her.

I saw her alone in her vineyards checking her crop of grapes. I couldn't resist. I just had to get to know her. So, I rushed from my motorcycle and I ran into the fields to see her.

"Ça va, mon ami?" (How are you my friend?)

"Quelle surprise!" Madeline exclaimed (What a surprise!), jumping up from a crouching position. "Votre ténacité portera bientôt ses fruits." (Your persistence will pay off soon.)

I couldn't describe how I was feeling, but I knew I was smitten with her. She was so beautiful, and I was becoming beguiled with her.

She was a statuesque beauty, a year or two older than me, perhaps about eighteen or nineteen years old. I never asked her age. A man never does. She took my breath away with her creamy complexion, soft brown eyes, and sultry auburn hair. I was falling in love with her.

Suddenly, a language barrier seemed to grow between us, and our conversation came to a standstill.

An eerie silence ensued until Madeline spoke up. "My dear friend, my English is certainly better than my German or your pathetic attempt at French." She decided to speak to me in English for the balance of our conversations.

Madeline told me that her family were long time owners of the winery and vineyard, La Vin Du Savoy, which occupied a large acreage in southern France. Madeline had the luxury of potentially inheriting a successful family enterprise with customers from all over Western Europe and the Mediterranean. They also had a significant number of overseas clients, including Americans. Their proximity to the French Riviera made it a logical stopover for hundreds of tourists every month.

As a result of her good fortune, Madeline had been able to attend private schools and study in several languages, including French, Spanish and Italian. Language issues were never a problem for Madeline while interacting with people from abroad and exchanging different currencies in her family's business, including French francs, Italian lira, Spanish pesetas and American dollars. While never alone, she did feel lonely at times. She was an only child. She had the company of her farm hands in the vineyards and winery, but that wasn't enough to satisfy her inner feelings and desires. She would always tell her parents that she would never get involved with the staff. When I came along, however, she saw something in me that might quench her inner craving.

"Mon chéri, je m'excuse mais je crois. . ." I began. (My dear, excuse me, I think. . .) Then in German and English I repeated myself, "Ich habe Gefühle für dich!" (I have feelings for you!)

"It's nice to finally know how you feel about me!" she said. "I'm not sure. Let me think about it for a while." Then she turned and walked toward the winery. I felt distraught and forlorn. I walked back to my motorcycle and returned reluctantly to headquarters.

Several weeks passed. By then it was the autumn of 1940. Cooler days were coming, although it never got too cool on the French Riviera. I was starting to think about Madeline again. I drove by her family's vineyard several times. If Madeline was there, I failed to notice her. I couldn't help myself. I remembered Heinz saying to me, "If you want it bad enough, then grab it while you can. Life is too short for regrets." I also recalled Heinz's other motto about no skirt being safe with him. I didn't think I had the prowess to be a ladies' man like Heinz, but I did not doubt the veracity of Heinz's assertions. Heinz was a true gentleman in every sense of the word. He told me that he was quite an athlete and an accomplished weightlifter in high school, so maybe he did have what it took to be a real "he-man." Well, that was Heinz, but it wasn't me.

My resolve hardened. I had to see Madeline again and express my feelings. It was late 1940, heading into 1941, early winter when I went to see her again. I drove up the vineyard's long driveway and saw her by the compound. She caught my eye. I rushed up to hug her. She gladly accepted my embrace. We kissed for several minutes.

"Qu'est-ce vous faites ici?" she asked. (What are you doing here?) "You're not one of them, are you?" she continued in English. She was so perceptive. She knew my heart and soul exactly by then. That's why I loved her.

"Who are you, really?" she asked. She sensed that I was really and truly on her side and not a Nazi spy, as my appearance suggested. Because of her extensive customer service experiences over the years and just being around hundreds of different people while growing up in her family's business, Madeline had developed a keen sense of human nature. Somehow, she just knew I wasn't who I appeared to be.

I loved my homeland. I really wanted Ukraine to be liberated from communist control. I had hoped that Germany would further my cause. Madeline sensed this and my cause.

"You're right," I admitted. "I'm not who I seem to be." Then I described my life story to her.

When I finished, she smiled and then asked me to come to the villa with her. We shared a glass of champagne and an afternoon of tender conversation, among other things.

I returned several times for more afternoon "conversations" until the reality of the war intervened once again. A telegram confirmed my next assignment. I would not see Madeline again.

Before leaving Madeline's villa for the final time, she said something to me that was quite prophetic, "Tenez-vous prêt à mener une action audacieux" (Get ready to do something exciting and daring). She was very perceptive. Somehow Madeline knew of the challenges that I would face soon. I couldn't help but love her for that vote of confidence in me. She was the true essence of love to me. I would never forget her.

I would find out what she meant if I didn't understand her exact words. Duty called. I was to be deployed to North Africa under Field Marshal Erwin Rommel.

Madeline would become just a fond memory for me because World War II once again reared its ugly head in my direction. Once more fear and uncertainty troubled me. What was to transpire next? What did this hideous Nazi regime–over time that was becoming more obvious to me–have to share now with its ignorant soldiers like me? Would the liberation of my homeland ever be realized? My experience in the war continued to unfold, this time in North Africa with the Afrika Korps.

Chapter 5:
Afrika Korps

I met with the regional commandant, Major Danzig, who said I was needed to lead a force in Libya under the command of none other than the "Desert Fox" himself, Field Marshal Erwin Rommel. I was truly honored beyond words at the prospect. I knew the reputation of this highly regarded hero, who had been one of the most revered and instrumental generals in the Western offensive, otherwise known as "blitzkrieg" or "lightning war." In less than six weeks, the Wehrmacht had overrun France, Belgium, and Holland, occupying most of Western Europe. It seemed there was no stopping them after that.

I graciously accepted the appointment. As I was leaving, however, the zone commander posed an important and perhaps curious question.

"Lieutenant Hrechko, you have demonstrated exceptional ability as an officer thus far, especially with your constant meticulous surveillance of this region on behalf of the Wehrmacht and the Third Reich, but I would like to know why you have been consistently late upon your return to home base in the evenings."

I shrugged. "I guess I was just too busy." I kept the real reason a secret, of course.

The next day I embarked to Libya aboard a German troop ship, which left Marseilles with hundreds of my comrades. It would prove to be yet another important turning point, not only in World War II but also in my life.

It was March 1941. The Afrika Korps landed in Tripoli, Libya, under Field Marshal Rommel. There was no time for fan fare. As a new lieutenant commander–I still couldn't believe it–I was placed in charge of a divisional unit. I caught a glimpse of the revered field marshal, but that was all. I was there for a purpose, a purpose I thought I would understand but which I was unable to reconcile with my own. If my beloved comrades and I hadn't faced warfare previously we were going to engage in it head on from that point forward.

My division marched east through Libya. Rommel led the way through Libya to a victory in Tobruk, which was not easy. The circumstances of success were not to the liking of the Afrika Korps' leadership. The ugly fighting conditions in the hot, dry desert coupled with the uncertainty of long supply lines made the eastern push into Libya and Egypt difficult. Also, while Germany was in Africa, supposedly to assist their so-called Axis partner, Italy, the larger goal for the Third Reich remained the invasion of Russia, at least according to Der Führer.

Without the cooperation of the Mediterranean countries, such as Greece, Yugoslavia and Bulgaria, the victories in North Africa were not assured. Despite the odds against Axis superiority, Rommel persevered with his quick lethal strike strategy.

I followed my hero's lead and persevered eastward. It was truly a battle of not only guns and artillery but also of wills and the incessant scorching heat of the Sahara desert.

As the days and weeks passed, the conditions of the African campaign exacted intolerable punishment to my division. Heat, a constant lack of water, and daily vehicle breakdowns quickly became the other enemies of the German forces. Daily battles also ensued at every oasis or water source where the Axis and Allies converged.

One time when our roop had gained a foothold at an oasis, we were able to spend a restful night. We talked for a while. I asked the guys how they were feeling. Almost in unison they replied, "Ich vermisse mein Zuhause." (I miss my home.) This was one of the last times that I talked with my troops.

Increasing troop numbers and the adaptability of British and other Allied land equipment turned the tables in favor of the Allies in the region. By mid-1942, when the U.S. forces boosted the numbers as well as the morale of the other Allies involved, it became increasingly obvious that running the war effort on several fronts, including Russia, the Mediterranean, and North Africa, was not in the best interests of the Third Reich. Germany was at a breaking point. An eventual Allied victory seemed inevitable.

Despite the increasing odds against us, I managed to press forward with my division.

I was steadfast in my resolve, however fleeting it was becoming in the midst of the uncertain campaign. I did manage to see my buddies from afar, despite everything else. Jan, Hans and Werner were in my division. I was certain that Heinz wasn't far behind. Those guys always seemed to stick together like glue.

"Wie geht es dir?" (How is it going?) I asked when I caught a glimpse of them. I didn't see much of them after that fleeting acknowledgement. It was probably one of the last times that I saw the three of them alive as a group. The ravages of war have the horrific effect of killing not only people but also friendships.

Following the German victory in Tobruk in May 1942, several campaigns in Libya caused the tide to shift from one side to the other as Axis and Allies struggled to gain the upper hand in the region. Many factors were instrumental in turning the tables in favor of an eventual Allied victory. Among them was the upbeat morale amongst the Allied forces due to America's involvement, which included additional personnel and equipment, following the Pearl harbour attack and America's subsequent declaration of war against Japan and Germany. Changes in Allied leadership with General Montgomery leading the British forces and General Esienhower leading the American forces provided additional impetus, as did Allied blockades and attacks on Axis supply lines and equipment depots.

With the lack of supplies and reinforcements, widespread disillusionment set in. Fatigue also played a role. We were all tired of fighting. By August 1942, the inevitable became increasingly obvious. Even Rommel knew it. He left unexpectedly prior to the Allied ambush at El-Alamein.

The vaunted Desert Fox was replaced by General Georg Stumme. The Allies had succeeded in surrounding the Afrika Korps at El-Alamein. Battles ensued for several weeks well into the autumn of 1942. Von Strumm was killed in action. El-Alamein proved to be the downfall of the Afrika Korps.

Even with Rommel's return in October 1942, retreat was the only option for the remaining forces of the Afrika Korps. Whether or not Rommel's leadership at El-Alamein could have made a difference was uncertain. The cards were stacked against the Nazis due to the overwhelming Allied forces. It seemed that the Desert Fox had had enough. While the reason for Rommel's departure from Egypt was uncertain. (In modern terms, it could have been described as PTSD–post-traumatic stress disorder), his return to Africa was short lived. He was immediately withdrawn prior to the retreat to Tunisia upon surrendering his troops in May 1943.

Thousands of casualties resulted from the final battles in Libya and Tunisia. Thousands more were captured. The remnants of the

Afrika Korps suffered greatly in their retreat including my division. Among the casualties was my good buddy, Jan, who was killed in battle right in front of me. The fate of my other pals was uncertain.

Once again I looked skyward and prayed to God, "What has become of my friends?" I asked the Almighty. For the first time in a long time, I began to cry. "Why God? Why?"

I had had enough of the war. Although my life had been spared, many of my compatriots were not so lucky.

I forced myself not to think about what had happened since I arrived in Afrika. Long marches, constant machine-gun fire, bayonets drawn, killing other soldiers who, like me, didn't want to die but had to be killed so that one or the other could kill again in battle. This was the horrible fact of war. After months in the hot dry Sahara desert, it was over.

Thousands of Germans and Italians surrendered and were unceremoniously marched across Libya and Tunisia westward toward the POW camps in Morocco, where they would serve out the remainder of the war.

For me the end of the North African campaign was a mixed blessing. I was lucky to be alive but I was devastated in so many ways. The long months of the campaign had aged me dramatically. Now a haggard veteran of war, I remembered a proverb I had heard somewhere.

"When we are young and lacking in life experience, all we have is a lot of luck going for us. When we are older and have plenty of life experience, we are lacking in luck." Indeed, luck had run out for the Afrika Korps. I didn't want to think about anything. I was alive, and that was all that mattered.

It seems that my cause had turned out to be nothing more than a pipe dream. Germany had failed on many fronts. The North African campaign, the Russian front, and the European theatre of battle were all lost causes. The Allies would eventually prevail. With that my hope for a liberated Ukraine was lost. The Soviet

Union would solidify its stronghold over the republics after the Allied victory in Europe. The Russians would also control much of Eastern Europe there-after.

Chapter 6:
POW (Prisoner of War)

With my life spared once again, I was starting to feel like a prover-bial cat with nine lives. Although I was one of thousands of POWs in the camps of Morocco, I was alive. I began to realize a change was occurring in me, a change that somehow renewed my outlook on life. Throughout my confinement in the POW camp, I became better acquainted with this transformation within me and how it would make me the better person I would become.

From time to time, however, I experienced flashbacks during my POW internment. I always thought of what I had endured as a sprite young man and how I had turned into a haggard war veteran. I remembered the inglorious last hurrah of the Afrika Korps at El-Alamein where the Germans were unceremoniously thwarted by a British and American ambush, rendering any aspi-rations of Nazi control in the region futile. I had also heard about the German defeat along the Russian front. It seemed that my own aspirations of a free Ukraine were also quashed upon learning of the outcome of that battle.

A nagging feeling of uneasiness persisted in my broken heart when I thought about my home and the people I loved. What had become of my friends and family in my beloved home village? What had become of the wonderful Gypsy family I met? What had become of Madeline? I had to get in touch with them somehow.

By then my English was fluent enough to enable me to speak to one of the POW guards whom I befriended.

"How does someone contact friends and family?" I asked.

"As a POW, under the terms of the Geneva Convention, you are allowed to send correspondences to friends and family through the International Red Cross," the guard replied. The Geneva Convention was an international protocol that protected the rights of POWs from all sides.

With the foregoing fresh in my overwhelmed and overwrought mind, I sat down with a pen and paper that I had managed to scavenge from the camp's garbage and wrote a letter to my parents and to the love of my life, Madeline. It took several days to put my thoughts and feelings on paper. I wrote with a gusto that I had never felt before. So much had happened since I left home and since I had last seen Madeline.

The POW guards and the camp commandant were gracious enough to forward my precious letter to my parents and to Madeline via The Red Cross. It would be many weeks before I received a reply. I would bide my time as I waited anxiously.

I made an important discovery while I was writing to my loved ones. I learned that I enjoyed learning. While scrounging in the garbage bins looking for paper, pens, and pencils, I picked up recent newspapers from London, New York, and Paris. I ravenously devoured them all. I enjoyed reading even though the news was not good for the Third Reich. Germany was failing, but didn't care about the Nazi regime anyway. It wasn't my concern in the first place. Its war machine had started to succumb to the Allied forces, especially after America made its presence felt. Many other strategic factors became clear to me while I was browsing through the headlines. I surmised that an Allied victory was inevitable. Was there still a faint hope for my homeland under the Allies? I wasn't certain about that either.

The intelligence game was another pivotal point leading to the Allied turnaround. The Allies had captured one of Germany's Enigma machines, which enabled them to break Germany's secret code machine and thwart Nazi missions. Many German air, sea, and land attacks were greatly curtailed before they could even get started. It was becoming obvious that world domination was not Germany's manifest destiny.

I continued to read daily news clippings with disgust. My reading not only broadened my outlook but also gave me a new sense of discernment and direction, increasing my thirst for knowledge. Each day my desire for new insights grew.

My comrades and the POW camp guards took notice of my interest in the written word. "Well, if it helps pass the time then go ahead and pursue your pastime," one of the guards said. It was more than a hobby though; it became an obsession.

As the days and weeks went by, I got to know the commandant on a friendly basis. He knew of my love of learning and lent me any book that I requested. I read anything that I could get my hands on. From short stories to poetry, I read as much as I could. Thanks to local libraries in Rabat, Casablanca and Marrakech, books were made available at the request of the POW camp.

With my increasing interest in world events, I was quickly becoming somewhat of a know-it-all around the camp. Soon my fellow prisoners were asking me for the latest news. It may have been the boredom and monotony getting to them, but I soon became the go-to guy for anything and everything of interest to them. In fact, I became the de facto camp leader, a beacon of hope and inspiration to everybody in the camp. My fellow prisoners also perceived me as a pillar of strength and knowledge. Even the guards seemed to take notice, their respect for me increasing by the day.

Day in, day out, the same crap masquerading as food found its way into the mess hall. The prisoners were desperate for proper nutrition. As I was somewhat of an authority figure among the POWs now, I spoke up about it one day. "I understand that under the Geneva Convention, prisoners of war are entitled to fair treatment, but what is happening with our food is inhuman. We are literally starving; something has to be done."

What ensued next was nothing short of a minor revolt. Trays, cups and whatever else was handy were thrown around the mess hall. The prison guards quickly put a stop to the rebellion. With pistol shots to the ceiling, a semblance of order was soon restored. Many of the POWs chose not to eat anything that day and for a couple days later. A hunger strike by a few adamant souls mushroomed into a camp-wide ordeal. As the unofficial leader of the POWs, I was summoned to the commandant's office.

"Lieutenant Hrechko, I've heard the prisoners' complaints," he said. "How do you suggest I solve the problem?"

"Sir, with all due respect, the prisoners deserve quality food. It's as simple as that."

"I'll see what I can do," he asserted. With that lukewarm response, I left his office and returned to my barracks in disgust.

The prisoners all knew there was better food in the camp's storerooms. A few of them watched the delivery trucks roll in on a daily basis, drooling over the delicious commodities that were unloaded. During our free time, some of the POWs, under my command and guidance, devised a plan to capture some of those tasty provisions. Daily watches were undertaken to determine delivery times and routines, including guard duty.

Then one day an opportunity presented itself to my group. The guards failed to secure the doors to the storeroom. Why was it left open? Frankly, we didn't care! That morning it was like the spoils

44

of war were waiting for us. It was our golden opportunity to attain the quality food that we desired and had been denied. Whether or not it was considered theft, we didn't care! We were hungry! We needed better food.

With the stealth of a modern guerrilla tactical force, we entered the storeroom and endeavored to claim what was legitimately ours. With a couple of POWs standing guard, minutes later we had grabbed enough meat, vegetables, and canned items to feed our group for several days. Unfortunately, with any successful mission comes complications.

Our plan had been a lost cause or so we thought at first. One of the camp guards on the far side of the pantry suddenly spotted us. He rushed over with his rifle, fully armed, and engaged. The guard yelled at us, "Hey! What the hell do you think you are doing?" Then, to our surprise, he continued in German "Was machen sie?"

We couldn't believe it, and we didn't know how to respond. We were desperately hungry and needed the food. The guard continued to yell at us in German. "Put that stuff back now!" he snapped.

"You spoke to us in German.," I said. " Why? How?"

The guard answered me in German, with an American accent. "Ich aus Amerika, von Milwaukee, Wisconsin. Ich verstehe Deutsch, spreche aber sehr wenig." (I am from Milwaukee, Wisconsin. I understand German but speak little.)

The guard thought about the situation a while, then spoke in a matter-of-fact fashion. "There will be consequences for this, but that will be up to the camp commandant to decide. Understood?"

"Jawohl! Ich verstehen," we replied. (We understand.)

Then, suddenly, the guard's attitude changed as if by divine intervention. "You know something?" he said, "I know what you guys have been through. I have seen how the cooks have been preparing your meals, and I understand that the food is not of the greatest quality. So, tell you what, guys: I'm prepared to look the other way. Just don't let me catch you here again, OK?"

Once he received our reassurance, the American guard smiled and introduced himself.

"My name is Corporal John Hinkle. I'm from Milwaukee, Wisconsin. I'm with the Forty-fifth Division of the US Army. My grandparents emigrated from Essen, Germany, in the early 1900s. My parents taught me to speak German at home. Of course, during the past few years they kept their language to themselves because of the threats to German-speaking people."

We all sighed after that. The relief and sense of joy we felt was indescribable. We had definitely made a new friend that day.

That night we all enjoyed the spoils of our misdeeds. Corporal Hinkle became our friend, but given the circumstances of the war, our relationship with him could be better described as a fellow comrade-in-arms. He talked to us from time to time about his home life. As a boy growing up in Wisconsin, he had been victimized because of his German ethnicity. "It wasn't easy to grow up in a state and a country where other people perceive you as a potential enemy. I was proud of my German background, but the other kids were constantly judging me as a threat to them. World War One heightened and intensified the prejudice my parents and grandparents felt," he added.

I realized I was also a victim of persecution. In fact, my entire homeland had been victimized. The Soviet regime, under the iron fist of Joseph Stalin, had undertaken mass pogroms and other atrocities against Ukraine. I remembered as a child hearing stories of mass starvations in Holodomor and Dukhobors protesting in the 1930s.

The plight of others became paramount in my thinking. The traumas that John Hinkle and I had endured were universal and not unique to any culture, or so it seemed. Sympathy for others began to germinate in my soul. I kept wondering about the people who were apprehended at gunpoint in downtown Paris and sup-posedly taken to evacuation camps outside of the city for their own "safety." I needed to know what actually happened to them. I kept asking questions and reading more about the war. I hoped that the missing pieces would fall into place and answer the questions that had plagued me since my days in France.

Over the next several months, John revealed more and more about himself to our receptive ears and open minds. We really enjoyed our frequent chats with him. John illustrated his burning desire to try to change himself or at least the perception of his background. While proud of his heritage, as a boy he vowed that he would become as American as he could. For starters, he became a boy scout and earned as many badges as he could. Later on he joined a local unit of the US Army Reserves to further reinforce his total Americanization process. While John didn't volunteer immediately following the Pearl harbour attack, duty called him to serve soon after his college graduation in the spring of 1942. John quickly rose in the ranks before he was deployed to North Africa, where he accepted a posting as a POW guard after serving on the front lines of the European theater for the past eighteen months.

Reinvention and validation were ideas that manifested themselves frequently in my search for identity. I was still very young. I realized I had made some mistakes, but I realized I was capable of change. The purpose I was seeking was well within my reach. I had to find it soon, and I would. I kept asking, "Why, God? Why, God? Why me?"

One day while I was checking books out to read in the camp's office, I found exactly what I was looking for: the Bible. Once I started reading it, I couldn't put it down for hours on end. It was a comforting friend, a source of inspiration and the sense of direction I needed. In the reference section I was able to find chapters about the various books of the Bible that directly related to my life and what was transpiring around me. For want of better words, it was a godsend to me.

The persecution of oppressed people, the killing of the innocent and the rampant racism and prejudices of the past, as described in the Bible's Old and New Testaments, resonated with my inner being. I realized that what I had witnessed in the European and North African theaters of World War II paralleled the crimes and horrors of the Bible. Through my daily readings and interpretations of the word of God, I gained not only an invaluable knowledge of history but also discernment and a sense of certainty that I had never known before.

Stories within the various books of the Bible unfolded before my open eyes and curious mind. The story of the Israelites' exodus from Egypt inspired me. This was why I was fighting. This was my cause. I wanted freedom for my homeland too. The reality of the war crystallized in my mind; however, the German cause under the Third Reich was a lost cause. Like the ancient Pharaohs of Egypt, I finally realized that Hitler was also a false leader and a false prophet. He was no demigod either. An entire nation had been fooled, and millions perished as a result of his propaganda.

My constant reading of the Lord's Book continued to transform me. In reading about the presentation of the Ten Commandments by Moses to the Israelites, I realized I was in no way a perfect man, but through my daily reading of God's Word, I gained immense knowledge and insights, and I was transformed into a new man. I realized that I loved God far more than anything else in my life. I knew it was God's love that had been with me throughout my young life. It was God who loved me and protected me whenever traumatic incidents occurred. Despite losing comrades and good buddies along the way, I was still alive thanks to my prayers and the protection of the Almighty.

"Danke schön, Gotte! Danke schön, Gotte!" I said. A total transformation continued to take place. Mentally, spiritually, emotionally, I became born again.

Hatred was no longer part of my personality. I had no place for it in my life. "Vengeance is mine, said the Lord" is what I learned from the Good Book. "Do good to others, love thy enemies," is what he read. There was no place for hatred in my heart and soul any longer. Still, there were things that made my soul ache. Despite reading God's Word, I was troubled to forgive others or certain life experiences and those experienced by my fellow countrymen. For instance, the violence and hostility against my people perpetuated by the Soviet Union troubled me to no end. The need to forgive those responsible for the mass atrocities ate at my soul. What I learned later about the mass roundups of thousands of innocent people throughout Europe by the Nazi regime–in an effort to remove certain people from the face of the earth, later called the Holocaust–horrified me and tested my faith in humanity. At war's end, revelations of the full extent of the horrors were disclosed to the world. The world would never forgive or forget ever.

Interestingly enough, my learning process started long before my imprisonment in Morocco. I had learned about cultural differences in the Middle East while I was a soldier in the Afrika Korps. I learned a couple of words in particular that aptly described the tensions of the region. One word, *nakba*, the Arabic word for "disaster", was seemingly juxtaposed with the Hebrew word, *rakhum*, which means "compassion." It was an interesting dichotomy, but they somehow resonated with me, given the region's history. It continues to be an undeniable and unalterable ambivalence of the human condition to this day.

As the weeks and months passed, I started to wonder if my letters to Madeline and my parents had ever been delivered. Then one day I received a letter from my beloved Madeline. Unfortunately, the camp commandant had to read every letter; there was still a war going on, after all. When I finally received it, with the zeal of a child opening up a gift at Christmas, I snatched the long-awaited letters and ripped them open.

I thanked God and the International Red Cross for safely returning the precious message to me, albeit several months after my initial letter to my beloved Madeline. I started reading feverishly. Her first few lines were in French, of course, since she was an attractive French woman. She also wanted to maintain an allure of romance, mystery, and beauty in her writing. My eyes glazed and my face brightened as I pictured her face while reading her long-awaited response.

"Cher Dmitri," she wrote, "tu me manques." (Dear Dmitri, you are missed.) "Ma chérie, je me souviens bien des choses en Provence avec toi." (My dear, I remember well the things in Provence, with you.) "Je suis désolé de ne pas avoir écrit depuis longtemps." (*I'm sorry for not writing in a long time.*) "Excusez-moi, mais je dois vous parler maintenant." (Excuse me, but I need to speak to you now.)

Then her mood in the letter changed, as did the remainder of her message. For a better understanding of her thoughts and feelings, she wrote in English.

"My dear, I didn't tell you something you should have known. I was using you. I was with and continue to be with the French Resistance. I was gathering intelligence on behalf of the Allies. I was working closely with the Free French forces in Marseilles who, in turn, passed on any intelligence to the British and the Americans."

I was aghast at her revelation but not entirely surprised because I had known her as a caring and compassionate soul, someone who would give her life for a just cause. However, I realized that maybe I didn't know her as well as I thought.

Mixed emotions and thoughts crept into my being. What do they say in French? "C'est la vie!" I shrugged as I reflected on the subject. They say the ones who love you the most will often hurt you the most. Another adage came to mind: "Familiarity breeds contempt." I didn't feel like that was the case with Madeline. After all, she cared about me, didn't she? I recalled reading famous adventure and romance novels. Many of those novels described how different it is to figure out the complexities of a woman's heart and mind. I thought about that for a while before reading on. Women are intriguing creatures, I surmised.

Whatever the circumstances of our eight-month romance, neither of us had ever surrendered anything of substance to the other side as far as military intelligence was concerned. (As a result of our combined ineptitude, neither the Allies nor the Axis powers were ever in jeopardy, thankfully.) In her letter, Madeline continued to reflect on how much my love meant to her despite the communication gaps that sometimes occurred between us.

Effective communication, it is said, is the key to conflict management. If there were problems between us, they weren't obvious. Sure, we were not always on the same wavelength, but something had held us together, and that something must have been love. As I reflected on our togetherness, I was certain that she cared about me. As I pictured her in my mind, with her radiant smile and her sultry, flowing auburn hair and tranquil brown eyes, I smiled to myself. She was pure joy and ecstasy in human form.

Having become a truly learned man, I wondered what all this meant to me. Madeline brought a joy to my life that I had never known before. She had reinvigorated my soul and re-energized my heart, a heart that had been lonely for the longest time.

Unfortunately, like most love affairs I had ever experienced, this one was enigmatic, to say the least. Much like the top secret Enigma machine, women required decoding to be properly interpreted and understood.

I sighed quietly as I finished Madeline's letter. I realized that she cared about me, but at the same time, she had a job to do.

I also realized that I had failed miserably at being a Nazi spy, but that didn't matter to me. I was never one of them anyway. Madeline knew that as well. "I knew you were not one of them and that you would never be one of them—a Nazi, that is," she said in her letter. I admired her insightful and perceptive nature and loved her genuine soul.

Then I scrambled to write a worthy reply to her insightful letter. While I knew that the possibility of seeing her again was slim, it was still a joy to read her loving thoughts.

Her last words to me were in her mother tongue, French, since she wanted to emphasize her femininity and also demonstrated her pride and confidence in me as a man.

"Ayez confiance en vous," she said. "Même. Les autres feront de mêmes." (Believe in yourself and so will others). I didn't completely understand, but I knew she was proud of me.

We continued to correspond for a short time longer. By the spring of 1944, however, our romance was over. World War II was also nearing its climax. The inevitable end was on the horizon.

Days and weeks turned into months. The camp routine became monotonous, and tensions were rising. The stifling heat of the Sahara Desert added to the feeling of unrest. Physical outlets were needed. These came in the form of frequent brawls between prisoners.

These brawls often started out as shoving matches before and during roll calls and then escalated into vicious scuffles with fists flying everywhere. While they enjoyed the fisticuffs, the camp guards eventually intervened to subdue the combatants. My leadership instincts once again took charge. Having observed the altercations between fellow inmates far too often over the previous weeks, I took the initiative to reinstate a sense of calm.

"Guys, guys, if you want to fight and work out your frustrations, let's try to make it a fair and equal competition, OK?"

There was a general consensus in response to my idea of holding a competition between prisoners. We would hold a competition to see who the toughest guy in the camp was.

A number of the strong, muscular fellows stepped forward to participate.

"All right, my friends," I said, "now we must prepare for the tournament. Let's get started." I put them through their paces and suggested that the thirty to forty contenders recall their basic training workouts and get themselves fit and ready for the tournament.

Over the next few days, the contenders went through various regimens of calisthenics and running. With the help of the camp commandant, the prisoners were also able to borrow equipment, which aided their workouts.

By the end of the week, the tournament was set to begin. A makeshift fighting ring was set up in the camp's courtyard. The first matches were set to begin immediately after the mid-afternoon chow call. I took charge of the entire proceedings. With the assistance of a few of my closest camp buddies, I created a schedule for the ensuing days of action.

Even the camp guards were excited to see the fights. They placed wagers amongst themselves as to who would become the champion. Some of the guards also wanted to see certain prisoners suffer some pain. A certain amount of animosity continued to linger between some of the prisoners and various guards despite the apparent goodwill that seemed to exist with this organized mayhem.

So it began. I took on the role of master of ceremonies and introduced the first round of competition.

"Welcome to our camp tournament, which will decide who is the best fighter in our camp," I began.

With that acknowledgement, the two most muscular men took to the ring and started sparring.

The first day of matches lasted well into the sunset hours. By day's end, sixteen survivors made it to round two.

The next couple of days saw more of the same type of battles, with the tougher guys usually winning their matches.

Enthralled by the brawling that was taking place, the guards wagered more and more amongst themselves. There were a few upsets, and some money was won by a lucky few. The betting continued over the next few days with even some American dollars finding their way into the hands of a few fortunate POWs who had some wherewithal to bet and cashed in on the odd upset.

Needless to say, there was a cry for more blood and gore by some of the callous spectators. As a conscientious supervisor, however, I never allowed things to get out of control.

Some matches lasted longer than others. The longest was over an hour in duration; the shortest less than a minute. The outcomes were rarely in doubt. The bigger, stronger guys usually won, but there were a few surprises.

The final day arrived. Who would be declared champion of the POWs? The finalists were scheduled to meet for the championship bout right after the midday chow break. The leading contender was Sergeant Gerhardt Mueller, a strapping, muscular man in his late twenties. His towering height of over two meters dwarfed just about every other fighter in the competition. So did his nasty attitude. He was the favorite to win the top prize and the glory of being declared Camp Champion. Not surprisingly, Sergeant Mueller was also known as the camp bully.

I was well aware of Mueller's reputation as a camp tough guy, but I tried to overlook that indiscretion.

I held the dubious distinction of refereeing the title fight. I just wanted to see a fair match with no one getting hurt. The prisoners and guards in attendance cringed at the thought of a possible mauling. However, the possibility of a blood bath was inevitable, given the size of the other participant and Mueller's past conflicts with fellow inmates. He had even come too close to comfort with a camp guard but hesitated when the business end of a rifle was pointed at his face.

The other contender did not quite measure up to Gerhardt in terms of stature, but he was no slouch either. Though slightly shorter, Corporal Franz Weiner still presented a formidable challenge. Like me and many others in the camp, Weiner came from humble beginnings, but he was a survivor due to his tenacity and winning attitude. After all, he had to defeat four other opponents to reach the championship round.

Immediately after midday chow call, the championship match was about to get under way.

"My friends, today we shall declare our Camp Champion," I said. "I will now introduce the contenders. On my right side, weighing about a hundred kilos, is Sergeant Gerhardt Mueller. On my left, weighing about eighty kilos, is Corporal Franz Weiner. Good luck, gentlemen." The two combatants shook hands and then went at it following the sound of a clanging pot, which served as our improvised bell.

Fists flew early on in the match. Mueller knocked Franz down several times during the first ten to fifteen minutes but the smaller fighter was able to sustain the ongoing punishment due to being in excellent physical condition. I had seen him jogging around the camp on a daily basis.

Thirty minutes into the fight, fatigue started to take its toll. Blood and sweat was dripping from the fighters' faces and upper torsos. It would not be an easy victory for either of them. The spectators were beginning to become as tense and frustrated as the fighters.

"Come on, schnell, schnell!" they yelled. "Let's go! Fight!"

After sixty minutes elapsed, the climactic conclusion was set in motion. Weiner, looking dejected by the continuous onslaught of Mueller's fists, put his head down in a momentary lapse of consciousness. It would be his undoing. With a decisive blow to the head, Weiner was knocked down and remained motionless for several minutes. With that blow, Mueller was declared the champion.

I raised the victor's hand and presented him with a makeshift championship belt made of an old frying pan and a burlap sack with the words "Camp Champion" printed on the pan.

"OK, everyone, we have our camp champion: Sergeant Gerhardt Mueller. Congratulations, Sergeant Mueller."

Perhaps it was the exhilaration of the match or maybe over stimulated hormones, but Mueller couldn't control his emotions. He slugged me with a right hook. "I'm the best!" Mueller declared, raising his arms in victory.

I clenched my jaw and then abruptly slugged Mueller back with a hard left. Shocked by the sudden retaliatory blow, he dropped to the floor. "You deserved that you SOB," I mumbled. Then I helped him to his feet and congratulated him once again with a handshake and a pat on the back. There were no hard feelings. The two of us actually became good friends over the following weeks, and I realized he wasn't really a bully after all.

Although Gerhardt portrayed the persona of a typical bully at first glance, I came to see that he was actually a very disciplined militaristic individual with a strong will. Brought up in a military family, he was focused on his career in the service. He never did things out of malice but rather in an orderly and disciplined fashion. He was a stickler for fitness–I often saw him working out in the camp's make-shift gym. I found out that the loss of his father earlier in the war had a devastating effect on him. His dad was a major who was killed in action. It had left a vacuum in Mueller's heart and soul. He wanted to live up to his father's honor.

There was more to Mueller than his tough outward appearance and seemingly gruff attitude. Through my relationship with him, I realized how much empathy resonated within me and others. It was another epiphany I learned a lot from Mueller and others like him. I couldn't be judgmental after that. Through my wartime and POW experience, I learned that life was too short to harbour hatreds or grudges. Forgiveness became important to me. Without forgiveness, there is no hope for love and compassion. I learned this for my own sake and very survival.

As we entered the spring of 1944, World War II was nearing its climax. The Allied forces were planning future decisive actions, culminating with D-Day in June and further break-throughs in Western Europe, with their eventual march toward Berlin.

As always, I kept busy reading and studyings. I even tried my hand at cooking for my campmates. With the help of our new friend, Captain Hinkle, the prisoners were able to enjoy more pilfered goodies from the camp supply stores. Out of sympathy, Hinkle didn't mind helping my pals and me with our badly needed "nutritional requirements" once in a while.

As it turned out, I was not a very good cook. My campmates often complained that my menu lacked a certain something called "flavour." While the food I cooked was certainly better than some of the crap they were normally served, it was still not up to the POWs' standards. What it boiled down to was that I had not per-fected the culinary art of seasoning and proper food handling. In fact, the prisoners in my section often complained that the Atlantic Ocean and the Mediterranean Sea had a lower salt content than some of my cooking. After a few too many complaints from my "customers," I threw in the towel as far as my cooking exploits were concerned.

Meanwhile, the war was still raging in the European and Asian theatres. The turning point was June 6, 1944, D-Day. While thou-sands of Allied soldiers were lost on the beaches of Normandy, the Allies gained a valuable foothold in Western Europe. Gradually, this foothold led to territorial gains and the liberation of Holland, Belgium and France. The Allied advances gained momentum as spring turned into summer.

A morale boost was needed by the Nazis in the form of the Hitler Youth. The propaganda campaigns of Nazi leadership had mesmerized these youngsters—many of them barely into their teens–turning them into a formidable fighting force. Unfortunately, enthusiasm and adrenaline were insufficient weapons against the Allied forces, who were determined to reach Berlin before the Soviet Union's Red Army got there.

Meanwhile, I kept reading the newspapers I had found. The camp commandant was kind enough to lend me the papers that arrived each day.

"Oh God!" I said to myself when I read the headlines. "It's God's will!" Judging by the stories I read, I knew the war would end soon.

"So be it," I thought. With that in my mind, my dream of a free Ukraine vanished.

Major battles were taking place in the Western front of the European theatre, including the infamous Battle of the Bulge in late 1944 and into early 1945. During this battle in Belgium, a major supply depot was destroyed, thus dislodging the German forces and forcing them to retreat eastward.

In the wake of the Germans retreat were the ruins of many villages and towns, torched by the Nazi soldiers. Thousands of civilian casualties were also the unfortunate results of the Nazi retreat. The Allied forces continued to push into the heart of the Third Reich. By May 1945, Europe was once again under the control of the combined Allied forces, which now included Italy, which had joined the Allies after the assassination of Benito Mussolini. Hitler had evaded certain capture and conviction by committing suicide along with several others, including his wife, Eva Braun.

On May 5, 1945, Berlin was surrounded, and Germany formally surrendered two days later. The war in Europe was over. The sombre revelations of the Nazi defeat and the Allied victory didn't reach the POW camp until several days later. There were no declarations of joy or disgust when the prisoners learned of the war's end. All that resonated throughout the camp was a death-like pall. Forbidding uncertainty prevailed.

Germany had been destroyed. Where were these POWs going to go now? Mass destruction throughout their homelands meant a bleak return to an unrecognizable shambles, if that. Communications between the front lines and the bewildered POW camps was tedious at best for the next while.

Like everyone else in camp, I was on edge. I asked the commandant for any news I could share with my fellow inmates. I learned that as of that moment, everyone was now considered "free" under the Geneva Convention.

In the coming days, information about the impending release of prisoners was forthcoming with the aid of the International Red Cross and various other groups, including the Allied forces.

Over the ensuing weeks, communication between the camps and *der Fatherland* revealed gruesome details, including horrible revelations from Eastern Europe regarding the discovery of the death camps as well as the destruction of many areas of Germany. With their homes destroyed, many POWs became known as displaced persons or DPs.

I realized it would be impossible for me to go home. I had betrayed the Soviet Union in joining the Wehrmacht and would almost certainly face a firing squad.

Those who were willing and able to return to their homes in Germany were given every opportunity to do so. For a significant number of others who were considered DPs, the most viable option available appeared to be transport to the new world, in particular, the USA and Canada.

"What will happen to me, dear God?" I prayed. Then I saw a firing squad in my mind's eye if I even considered returning to my Ukrainian village.

The final days of camp life arrived. A melancholy ambience pervaded the final assembly and roll calls in my section. As I recalled the battles in North Africa, I remembered watching the death of one of my buddies right in front of me. Jan Smigler was killed during the advance into El-Alamein, but what became of Heinz, Werner, and Hans? Those three guys usually stuck together with me, but I had not seen them since El-Alamein.

After the hour-long roll call, I presented myself to the head of the POW guards and inquired as to the whereabouts of my three friends.

"Sergeant, do you have any record of Werner Klump, Hans Eisch, or Heinz Schultz?" I asked.

The sergeant checked his record book for information, flipping through several pages. Then he finally looked up at me.

"Lieutenant, I'm so sorry to have to tell you this, but Werner Klump and Hans Eisch both died of their war injuries a few weeks ago. I am so sorry for your loss. They were good friends of yours, I assume?"

"Yes, they were very good friends of mine," I replied.

"But I do have some good news for you," the sergeant said.

My ears perked up.

"Heinz Schultz is still alive and well. You will find him on the other side of the camp, across a set of railroad tracks, in the south section of the facility." He pointed out the way across the compound where I could find my old friend, Heinz.

I hurried across the compound and opened a gate that led into the south section. I looked across a set of railroad tracks to see if I could spot my longtime pal in the crowd of dispersing POWs. As I was searching for Heinz, my mind flashed back to when we first became acquainted and the good times we had together. Heinz wasn't the least bit shy about those fun times. After all, he always said that "no skirt was safe" around him. I knew he meant that in fun. He was never evil in mind or soul. He was too nice of a guy. He was my best friend, without a doubt. I reflected on all the poker games and the drinking joints we frequented. Heinz didn't always play fair, but he did win his fair share. I chuckled to myself as I recalled the Luger pointed at Heinz. As far as drinking was concerned, no one could drain a bottle of lager or schnapps faster than Heinz. As a result of his alcoholic prowess, Heinz had won many drinking competitions.

Using my hand to shield my eyes from the sun, I finally spotted Heinz in the distance and waved enthusiastically at him. My longtime pal recognized me and waved back. We ran toward each other with the eager anticipation of a warm embrace. However, I stopped short of the first set of railroad tracks when I heard an oncoming freight train round the bend. Heinz appeared to be unaware of the train and kept running toward me.

I tried in vain to halt Heinz's progress by waving for him to stop, but it was too late. In the delirium of his excitement, Heinz didn't notice the train, and it struck him. The impact threw Heinz several metres across the compound. The scene was palpable. My best friend from the last several years was gone in an instant. I realized I had just lost not only a friend but also part of my soul. Guards and prison officials were quickly on the scene to retrieve the body. Devastated, I fell to my knees. "Why, God? Why?" I cried. A part of my died that day. Grief took hold of my being. I wept for days on end non-stop.

Days passed, and the reality of war's aftermath continued for the remaining former POWs, now considered DPs or refugees. I contemplated my next move. I couldn't stay there: that was for certain.

We received more news from Allied-occupied Germany. In its push toward Berlin from the east, the Red Army had made the grisly discovery of massive death chambers in Eastern Germany and Poland. The names of Auschwitz, Dachau, Treblinka, and many others would resonate throughout the world forever. These extermination camps, the Nazis' so-called Final Solution, had decimated the lives of some six million Jewish people and countless others.

Upon reading and hearing these reports, I couldn't bear to deal with such a horrible and catastrophic turn of events. Europe and the world they thought they had known was in shambles. We decided amongst ourselves that we would go to the new world. "I'm going to America!" I declared. With this new direction in mind and a steadfast conviction renewing my life, I looked forward to a new chapter and a new beginning. My new cause was a new life in the new world. From then on, Ukraine would only be a fond memory.

Chapter 7: A New Beginning

An array of troops and freight ships arrived along Morocco's Atlantic coast. The ships were hired to transport the hundreds of former POWs to resettlement camps in the US and Canada.

Along with my fellow campmates, I eagerly awaited the instructions from our higher-ups as to when we could embark on our epic journeys to the new world.

The voyage would take several weeks, but that didn't matter. "I will start over in America," I consoled myself. Others shared similar thoughts as we assembled our few meager possessions for our journey to freedom.

As we boarded the freighter, I turned back toward the camp and northward toward Europe and reflected on where I had come from and what I had learned over the past few years. I also recalled a quote that I had read: "Life isn't measured just in the air that we breathe but rather what we put into those moments of life." The things that capture our imagination and literally take our breath away are what stimulate us to continue our life journey. I smiled to myself. Then I looked skyward and thanked the Almighty for his constant love and support.

During the trans-oceanic crossing, I pretty much kept to myself, contemplating and studying a Bible that the camp commandant had graciously given to me.

I had realized I had made a few good friends at the POW camp. I really had no enemies now. I remembered what I had read in the Bible at times of distress.

"Oh God, please help me. Let thy enemies be scattered."

As the freighters approached the shores of North America, I was still anxious to know the fates of my family members and friends back home.

Despite the uncertainty of my loved one's fates, I consoled myself with the thought that I had gained a lifetime of experiences and learned invaluable lessons over the past six years. This realization overwhelmed me. For instance, through my steadfast dedication and devotion to my cause and my ongoing duties as a good soldier, important markers of my character and my personality were instilled in me.

Among these markers were the qualities of love, tolerance, gratitude, charity, hopefulness, faith and respect for oneself as well as others. Above all I discovered the most important lesson in my life: the joy of being alive despite the sometimes dire and horrific circumstances of life. *This is the grace of God,* I reflected.

A few days later I ventured onto the ship's main deck to view the skyline of New York City. It was an unimaginable sight, one that I thought I would never see. The fabled and iconic Statue of Liberty came into my view soon after.

When I looked at the torch of liberty, I realized I was one of those thousands, if not millions, of immigrants and refugees who had made the brave trek to freedom in the new world in a search for a better life. The inspired words emblazoned on the pedestal of Lady Liberty resonated with me. I was one of the people mentioned, most assuredly. I smiled to myself and again thanked God for bringing me to new opportunities and a new life. "Thank you, dear God!"

"Yes, Lord, I'm one of your people. I am truly grateful to be here and grateful for your love."

Then I thought about my new American friend, John Hinkle. Milwaukee, Wisconsin can't be too far away from New York City, I thought.

I decided right then and there that I would go visit him.

When we reached the arrival point at Ellis Island, I reached down and kissed the ground and again expressed my gratitude for my life.

"Thank you, God!"

Later on during my stay at a resettlement camp in upstate New York, I finally made contact with my family back in Ukraine. I learned my parents had returned to our old farm. Things weren't exactly the same, but they were generally well. I was happy and grateful to learn of their well-being.

After a quarantine period and a probationary period of confinement, I was allowed to travel freely. I got in contact with John, and he agreed to meet me at Grand Central Station in New York.

"It's good to see you again, my friend," I said as I embraced him, tears running down my face.

I was John's guest at his home in Milwaukee for several days. We spent the time reminiscing and talking about our families. I was the happiest I had been in a long time.

John wanted me to meet someone, a middle-aged woman. This person was someone that I thought I would never have the opportunity to meet. This middle-aged woman was Sophie Kirschov. She was a Holocaust survivor.

Although the fortuitous meeting occurred several months after the war's end, the horrible memories of the death camps were still vivid in Sophie's mind. She was one of the fortunate few whose

American relatives saved her from the trauma of the Holocaust. Sohpie's family were friends of the Hinkles in Milwaukee. Although hesitant at first, Sophie eventually opened up about her experiences in the death camps. I assured her that I understood what she had gone through. I revealed my own circumstances to her. She was shocked at first but understood my cause. "I didn't like the Russians either," she said as she reflected on her family's early life in the Soviet Union prior to their immigration to eastern Germany in the 1920s.

Sophie sighed to herself. After a few moments of deep reflection, she revealed what she had witnessed in Treblinka. Sophie also rolled up her left sleeve, revealing a tattoo of a long series of numbers. It was her registration number in Treblinka. "It was because I was useful to the Nazis," she said in a strong Yiddish accent. "That's why they kept me alive. I also did some gardening, and I was a musician. I could play the violin. When the naked people were herded into the gas chambers, they thought they were going to take showers, but I heard the screams from inside when the doors closed." Tears ran down her face. "I knew what had happened, but I had to keep quiet every time, or else they would kill me too. I was spared. But the Nazis murdered my entire family." Her hands then covered her weary eyes. She continued to sob as she related the horrors she had witnessed. It was one of the few times she had talked about her experiences to anyone. John's family was one of the first few who were unsettled by her stories.

I thanked her for telling her story to me. "It's OK," I consoled her, "you don't have to tell me any more." I hugged her and told her that I loved her.

"My friend, we should go now," I said to John. "This should never have happened. Why, God? Why?"

Later that night I had dinner with John and his family. I reflected on what I had learned that day from someone who had lived the horrors of an evil undertaking in the Holocaust. I was also a survivor and a witness to the demented and despotic regimes under evil leaders, namely Stalin and Hitler. I had long since vowed to never allow hatred and prejudice to enter my psyche or become part of my life.

I stayed the night with John's family. I said goodbye to him the next morning and returned to New York. We kept in touch over the years.

On my return train trip to New York, I couldn't help but reflect on where I had come from. My mind flashed back to my early years. I remembered my boyhood in Ukraine. I remembered my good pals. I wondered what they are doing now. Was Maria happy? Where was Madeline? Did she find love? The experiences, the places, the relationships, I was honoured to have all contributed to who I have become. What would become of me? I love country life. Would I become a farmer like my Tati? Hmm. I gripped my chin and thought about that for awhile.

Years later I became what my parents wanted me to become: a farmer. I enjoyed the countryside, so I settled into American life as the manager of a small farm in the Connecticut countryside. My neighbours were not friendly with me at first, but over time they came to respect my family and me. My children learned about World War II in school and were anxious to ask me about my younger years. As inquisitive teenagers they wanted to know everything about me. My three kids–one girl and two boys–were as curious as I was when I was their age.

"Father, is it true that you fought against evil in the war?" my youngest son, Daniel, aged ten, asked.

"With conviction," I said. "My son, sometimes in life when you choose to fight for freedom, you have to commit to that cause. For me that cause was for the freedom of my boyhood home, Ukraine. Daniel, my son, I didn't know what I was getting myself into then, but I believed in my heart that it was the right thing to do."

My oldest son, John, aged twelve, and my daughter, Amy, aged eight, wanted to know why I fought with the Germans. Why couldn't America help my cause? I answered them with a contrite heart. "Children, I guess I didn't know any better. I was just a naïve teenage boy. We learn a lot from our mistakes, don't we? What I learned is that the Germans were just as evil as the Soviets, who were holding my beloved Ukraine captive. My children, I have learned what is truly most important in life. It's love! We must love one another. If I had not fallen in love with your mother (Anne, my beloved wife of over fifteen years), I would have never had the incredible experience of loving three wonderful children."

"We love you too, Daddy," my kids said as we all embraced in a group hug. I love my family. I love my life now. It is wonderful.

Many questions had been answered in my mind. Life is an amazing story, isn't it? Without turmoil, one won't recognize peace, just as without rain, there certainly cannot be flowers or rainbows. Life is what you make of it. For me, it was an amazing story. I don't believe I could have lived it any other way. Thank you God!

Epilogue

An unknown philosopher once said, "Life has a way of finding us, whether we like it or not".

In Dmitri Hrechko's amazing story, his life truly found him. He came from humble beginnings and faces a calamitous world situation head on with the determination and fortitude of a man much older than his teenage years.

Enduring pain and hardship with the nobility of a great soldier and servant loyal to the cause he sought: freedom for his beloved Ukraine - he fought for what he believed was right. Grief, tragedy and the horrors of a war were his constant companions throughout but Dmitri persevered. At the end, he found the joy and love he longed for.

With faith, inner strength, an insatiable curiosity and zest for life, Dmitri attained true greatness and gained the admiration he deservedly earned.

His, was indeed, an 'Amazing Story'.

Final Thoughts

It was a joy to write this story. While countless hours went into the writing, I considered it an enjoyable labor of love. The story, while one of fiction, was based upon many conversations and reminiscences with family and friends over the years. Suffice it to say, many people in my life would not be alive today without the past experiences of one Dmitri Hrechko.

Finally, we are human. We have to remind ourselves of this question: "Why are we here?"

As human beings, we are all here for a purpose. God instills in each of us that divine purpose. It is up to us to ascertain and fulfill that purpose. Dmitri Hrechko fulfilled that purpose that was bestowed on him. Despite not achieving the freedom he vowed for his homeland, he nevertheless became a better man.

Therefore, pray everyday and earnestly study the Bible and find your purpose.

Thank you and may God Bless.

A Final Prayer
(illustrating Dmitri's character)

Blessed is the one who trusts in the Lord,
Whose confidence is in Him.
They will be like a tree planted by the water that
Sends out its roots by the stream.
It does not fear when heat comes; its leaves are
Always green.
It has no worries in a year of drought and
Never fails to bear fruit.

Jeremiah 17:7-8

References

Literature

1. Ullrich, Volker. (2020) *Downfall 1939-1945*. Translated by Jefferson Chase. New York, NY: Alfred A. Knopf.

2. Shirer, William. (2011) *The Rise and Fall of The Third Reich: A History of Nazi Germany*. 15th edn. New York, NY: Simon and Shuster.

3. *Collier's Encyclopedia: Erwin Rommel, World War II. vol. 20 & 23*. (1969) Crowell-Collier.

Historical Movies

1. Attenborough, R. (Director). (1977) *A Bridge Too Far* [Film]. Joseph E. Levine Productions.

2. Ayer, D. (Director). (2014). *Fury* [Film]. Columbia Pictures, QED International, L-Star Capital.

3. Curtiz, M. (Director). (1942) *Casablanca* [Film]. Warner Brothers.

4. Korda, Z. (Director). (1943) *Sahara* [Film]. Columbia Pictures.

5. De Laurentis, D. (Director). (1965) *Battle of the Bulge* [Film]. Warner Brothers.

Acknowledgements

I am greatly indebted to the many family members and older friends who have contributed their reminiscences. They have enlightened and inspired me to write a captivating and adventurous novel.

I am also grateful to the many collaborators who have assisted me in this work including my publishing advisors. Also a big 'Thank You' to my personal advisor at Friesen Press. Thank you Cam Bradley.

I am truly grateful to all of those I have not mentioned who have contributed to this novel. I am also thankful to those who have enjoyed reading it. May God Bless you all!!!

Finally, a huge thank you goes toward one UPS Store associate, whose tireless efforts contributed significantly to the book project. Thank you Adam Cwiok from The UPS Store.

Printed in Canada